Sprocket's Christmas Tale

By Louise Gikow
Pictures by Lisa McCue

Muppet Press
Holt, Rinehart and Winston
NEW YORK

Copyright © 1984 by Henson Associates, Inc.
Fraggle Rock, Fraggles, Muppets, and character names are trademarks of Henson Associates, Inc.
All rights reserved, including the right to reproduce this
book or portions thereof in any form.
Published by Holt, Rinehart and Winston,
383 Madison Avenue, New York, New York 10017.

Library of Congress Cataloging in Publication Data
Gikow, Louise.
Sprocket's Christmas tale.
Summary: Gobo Fraggle and Sprocket the dog each
have a special wish for Christmas, and on Christmas
morning both wishes come true.
[1. Puppets—Fiction.   2. Christmas—Fiction]
I. McCue, Lisa, ill.   II. Title.
PZ7.G369Sp   1984   [E]   84-6526
ISBN: 0-03-000708-9
First Edition
Printed in the United States of America
1 3 5 7 9 10 8 6 4 2

ISBN 0-03-000708-9

CHAPTER ONE

SPROCKET was having a bad time.

It was the evening of December 24, and as most dogs know, that meant it was the night before Christmas. The radio was playing Christmas carols, and there was a big Christmas tree in Doc's workshop. For weeks Sprocket had been searching for a very special present to put under that tree. Now time was running out, and he had a big problem on his paws.

He hadn't decided what to give Doc for Christmas.

Last Christmas it had been easy. Sprocket had been walking down the block a few weeks before the holidays when he noticed a wonderful old hammer sticking out of a box of discarded tools. Thinking quickly, he had grabbed it in his teeth and headed for home. Doc had needed another hammer, and the present had been a great success.

This season Sprocket wanted to outdo himself. After all, he and Doc had been together for a lot of Christmases. But Sprocket hadn't been able to find anything nice enough. And now it was almost too late.

Sprocket looked over at the Christmas tree and sighed. It was an unusual tree. A few days before, Doc had gone looking for the Christmas-tree ornaments. By the time he was finished, he had unpacked every box and carton in the workshop. But there were no ornaments to be found. So Doc had done the best he could. The Christmas tree was hung with lots of old tools, a red woolen muffler that Doc's mother had knit for him, and a blue woolen muffler that she had knit for Sprocket. Doc had even hung some of Sprocket's dog biscuits on the tree.

Doc's present for Sprocket was already lying there, wrapped in shiny gold paper and tied with a red ribbon. Sprocket just *knew* it was something wonderful, but he had nothing to give Doc in return.

Sprocket felt terrible.

Earlier that day, Doc had gone out to pay his annual visit to his old Boy Scout troop. Each year all the old Boy Scouts got together on the day before Christmas and talked a lot about the good old days. They drank punch and tied lots of knots and told stories about all their adventures in the woods. Then they all sang Christmas carols.

But Doc would be home soon now, and Sprocket would have to greet him with empty paws.

Suddenly the music on the radio stopped, and a news bulletin came on. "Flash!" said the announcer. "The major snowstorm we are having will cover the entire area with over two feet of snow! Don't expect to go anywhere tonight, folks. Buses and trains will probably stop running, and they won't finish clearing the streets till tomorrow. I hope everyone is already home. Merry Christmas, and good evening."

Oh, no! Sprocket rushed to the window. Sure enough, big white flakes were whirling down, covering the mailbox and the steps outside the house. Sprocket could barely see out to the sidewalk. He would never be able to find a present for Doc now. And Doc probably wouldn't even make it home tonight!

Sprocket curled up in his basket, hungry and upset. Not having a present for Doc was bad enough, but spending Christmas Eve alone was worse. Burying his nose under his blanket, Sprocket drifted off into a troubled sleep.

CHAPTER TWO

ABOUT five feet away from where Sprocket was snoring, there was a medium-sized hole in the baseboard of Doc's workshop. And if Sprocket had been small enough to crawl through the hole, he could have traveled down long tunnels and twisty passages and mysterious caves...and discovered the world of Fraggle Rock!

Luckily for the Fraggles, he couldn't. Most Fraggles only come up as high as Sprocket's nose, and a big, barking dog is not a Fraggle's idea of a pleasant companion.

Actually, in some ways, Fraggles are a little *like* dogs. For one thing, they have tails. And they are sort of fuzzy, like dogs, but their fur comes in far more interesting colors—blue and red and pink and yellow and green.

Fraggles also spend most of their time playing, which dogs often do. But Fraggles play much more interesting games than dogs, games like Fraggle Freeze and Bop Ball. Fraggles also love to swim in the pool in the Great Hall of Fraggle Rock. And that's where Gobo Fraggle was right now.

Gobo Fraggle is known throughout Fraggle Rock as an adventurer and explorer. He has been to mysterious caverns and distant places that no other Fraggle has seen—except for his Uncle Traveling Matt. Gobo's Uncle Matt is probably the greatest Fraggle explorer of all time. He is currently exploring Outer Space, which is the Fraggle term for our world—yours and mine and Sprocket's. He sends Gobo postcards that describe all his adventures. Someday Gobo hopes to follow in his uncle's footsteps.

But right now Gobo wasn't doing any exploring. In fact, he wasn't doing much of anything except thinking. It was the time of the Fraggle Rock Winter Festival, which is usually a happy time for all Fraggles. But Gobo was feeling a little gloomy, and the reason for his gloom was his Uncle Traveling Matt. This would be the first Winter Festival that Matt would spend away from his nephew. And even though Gobo had a lot of special friends in Fraggle Rock, the thought of being apart from his uncle during the holidays made him very unhappy indeed.

All around Gobo, Fraggles were decorating the Great Hall. They were hanging cave moss and colorful vines, and drawing lots of pictures. The Fraggle Winter Festival isn't like our Christmas, but it does begin around the same time, and it is celebrated in similar ways—with presents and games and laughter and friends and family.

Fraggles love holidays. They also have a spring holiday, a summer holiday, a fall holiday, and a special movable holiday that they can celebrate whenever they feel like it—which is almost all the time.

But Gobo wasn't feeling much like celebrating. He dangled his toes in the water. He hated sitting around, but he couldn't think of anything he wanted to do.

"I know!" he suddenly said out loud to no Fraggle in particular. "I'll go to the hole and see if my Uncle Traveling Matt has sent me another postcard! Getting a postcard won't be as good as actually seeing him, but it's something!"

Gobo jumped up and headed toward Outer Space—and Sprocket—at a fast trot.

And where was Sprocket while all this was going on? He was safe in his basket, fast asleep, dreaming about Christmases gone by. . . .

CHAPTER THREE

THE first part of Sprocket's dream was not a happy one. He was dreaming of the time when he was a little puppy. Sprocket had been born in a back alley in a cold and dismal part of town. His bed had been a pile of old rags. He hardly remembered his mother, and he had been alone for a long, long time. In his dream, Sprocket was barely eight weeks old, and the world was not a particularly nice place to be.

In Sprocket's dream it was blowing and snowing outside, and Sprocket was hungry. He trotted out to the corner to see if there was something to eat in the trash can. All along the street, lights were on in the houses, and he could see groups of human beings inside. Sprocket had never met a human being, but the Old Dogs had told him about them.

"They mean well, I suppose," Ten-Spot Tom had once said. "But sometimes they can't see three inches in front of their short, useless noses! Some of us dogs have to look out for them and take care of them. Not me, of course." Tom sniffed. "It's a wandering life for this old dog. But you never know. One day maybe you'll adopt a human being your-self. Most of us do."

Suddenly Sprocket heard voices. He poked his nose out from behind a building and saw the nicest human being he had ever seen! The human being was ever so tall and was wrapped in a big scarf and wore red woolen mittens. He was talking to another human being in a blue uniform, and Sprocket suddenly stopped short. Uh-oh! Tom had warned him about *this* kind of human being.

Suddenly the human being in the uniform shouted something and pointed right at Sprocket! Sprocket barked one small, terrified bark and started to run. The human being chased him up one street and down the other. Sprocket's short, stubby legs started to get tired, and his breath came in quick pants. And then before he could do anything, a big net scooped him up in the air. He was captured!

Sprocket dangled in the air. He knew it was all over. He had heard the stories that the Old Dogs told late at night, of puppies who had gone for a walk and then never returned. The two human beings, meanwhile, seemed to be barking loudly at each other and waving their front legs in the air. It was all very confusing and frightening, and Sprocket began to whimper.

At that moment the nice-looking human being reached into the net and picked Sprocket up. The human being made some quiet, soothing noises in his throat, and then he started to scratch Sprocket behind the ears.

Sprocket was in heaven! He wriggled happily in the human being's paws. And then Sprocket looked into the human being's eyes, and the human being looked back at Sprocket, and somehow it was decided. That was how Sprocket had chosen Doc. And Sprocket had never regretted it.

Sprocket grinned in his sleep. What a nice day *that* had turned out to be! The dream went on. Now it was Sprocket and Doc's first Christmas together. Sprocket had never heard of Christmas until Doc told him about it. Actually, Sprocket thought it was a great idea—a holiday on which everybody showed everybody else how much they loved them by giving them presents.

Sprocket particularly liked the presents part. That first year Doc gave him a wonderful chewy bone, and he gave Doc an old woolen sock that Doc had lost behind the radiator. The next year, Doc gave him a bright red rubber ball, and he gave Doc an old black umbrella with spokes that stuck out all over the place. And that was the way it had been—wonderful presents and fun! Until now. . . .

Sprocket whimpered in his sleep. Somehow his nice dreams were turning sad. He suddenly found himself on a long, white road with snow falling all around. He was running and running, which was getting harder and harder as the snow got deeper. He didn't know where he was going, but he knew there was something he had to do. He just couldn't remember what it was! He only knew he had to keep on going. . . .

"Woof!" Sprocket woke up in a rush. He still felt a little out of breath from his dream run. Where had he been running to? There was something he had to do, and he couldn't remember. . . .

He looked around for Doc, and then he suddenly knew. Doc's Christmas present! He still didn't have one. And then Sprocket remembered the snowstorm, and what the radio announcer had said. He looked up at the clock. It was almost midnight. Doc would never make it home tonight.

Sprocket hid his head under his paws and moaned. No Doc and no present. It was almost unbearable. What was he going to do?

CHAPTER FOUR

As Sprocket lay there feeling miserable and lonely, he heard a commotion outside the workshop door. First there was some muffled muttering, and then a lot of shouting. Then there were a bunch of thumps, followed by some scraping sounds. Finally the door opened wide—and in came Doc. He was covered with snow from head to foot!

"Sprocky! Boy, am I glad to be home!" Doc cried. "I thought I'd never make it. The snowplows only got as far as Ned Shimmelfinny's house, and he had to lend me a shovel so I could dig my way here." Doc stamped his feet to shake some of the snow loose. Then he reached over and closed the door.

But before he did, a small figure snuck into the workshop behind him.
The figure was about as high as Doc's knee. It was wearing a backpack
and a funny hat, and walking with the aid of two red-and-white-striped
walking sticks.

Sprocket's eyes opened wide. *Hey, it's a Fraggle!* he barked. *Doc, look!
There's one of those Fraggles I've been telling you about! Look, look! Over
there!*

"Sprocket! What are you barking about, boy?" Doc laughed, turning to
hang his coat on the radiator to dry. "I'm glad that you're happy to see
me, but calm down! I'll be right with you!"

No! Sprocket barked. *Look now! It's one of those Fraggles! See?* Sprocket hopped out of his basket in the direction of the Fraggle, who was heading for the hole as fast as he could.

Hey, Fraggle! Sprocket barked, running toward the Fraggle. *Wait a second! I want Doc to see youuuuuuuuu.* . . . And Sprocket made a dive for the Fraggle. If only he'd stay a moment. Then Doc would know what Sprocket had been barking about all these months!

But all the Fraggle heard was "Woof woof, bow wow, ruff ruff!" And all he saw was a very large, very anxious furry Beast rushing toward him! The Fraggle ran for the hole as fast as he could. In his rush to get there, he dropped his two red-and-white walking sticks.

Sprocket skidded past the sticks and reached the hole just as the Fraggle's tail was disappearing through it. He grabbed with his paw, but missed. *Oh, cat's whiskers!* he barked. *Doc will* never *understand!* And then Sprocket's mouth fell open. Doc! Doc was back! And there was no present for him! Oh, no!

Time had run out for Sprocket.

CHAPTER FIVE

GOBO had just turned the last corner of the tunnel that led to Outer Space when he bumped head-first into the Fraggle who had run from Sprocket.

"Uncle Traveling Matt!" Gobo cried in astonishment. For that, in case you haven't guessed, is who the Fraggle was!

"Hey! Watch out, you young—why, it's my Nephew Gobo! How are you, Gobo?"

"Uncle Traveling Matt!" Gobo cried again. "I was just going to look for a postcard from you. What are you doing here? Welcome home!"

The bump turned into a hug. Matt patted Gobo on the back, and Gobo patted Matt on the backpack.

"I decided I didn't want to spend the holidays all alone out there," Uncle Traveling Matt explained. "I missed you, Nephew, and I missed Fraggle Rock. But you'll never guess what happened on my way back here! It was almost my most exciting adventure of all time!"

"Wow," breathed Gobo. "Tell me all about it!"

Traveling Matt shook his head. "It's a miracle that I got here at all. First, there was a terrible snowstorm! The snow was so deep, I could hardly move! And the wind was so strong, it kept blowing me over!"

"There are weird Snow Creatures in Outer Space," Matt went on. "One giant creature seemed to want to play. He kept throwing snow around from one place to another. But he didn't see me, and he almost buried me alive!

"Soon I got to a place where the snow was so deep that I couldn't walk at all. I was going to give up! But then I saw the Silly Creature who lives outside the hole. He seemed to be headed in this direction, and he was moving the snow out of his way as he went. So I followed him until I got inside. And then the Beast attacked!"

Gobo knew the Beast well. Sprocket was there every time he collected one of Traveling Matt's postcards.

"I was almost at the hole when he charged!" Traveling Matt shuddered. "He made terrible noises and grabbed for me. It was horrible!

"But the worst thing of all," Matt sighed, "is that I was bringing you a wonderful Winter Festival present, and the Beast made me drop it. It was a beautiful red-and-white walking stick. I had one exactly like it. In Outer Space, the Silly Creatures use certain large plants for storage. They hang all sorts of useful items on them, like balls and things to eat and these walking sticks.

"But both sticks are gone now. I'm sorry, Nephew Gobo. I wanted to bring you a special gift from Outer Space for the holidays."

Gobo shook his head in admiration. "It doesn't matter about the present, Uncle Matt," he said. "*You're* my present! Having you home is going to be the best part of the Fraggle Rock Winter Festival! Come on, now! Let's tell everyone you're back!"

Gobo put an arm around his uncle's shoulders, and the two of them headed happily off to the Great Hall of Fraggle Rock.

CHAPTER SIX

B<small>Y</small> the time Doc had finished taking off his boots, Uncle Traveling Matt had long since disappeared, and Sprocket's barks had turned to whimpers.

"Hey, Sprocky," Doc said, "you sound upset. What is it, boy?" Sprocket just groaned.

Doc scratched Sprocket's head, frowning. Then he slowly nodded his head.

"You were afraid I wouldn't get home in time for the holiday, weren't you, boy?" Doc said, rubbing the special place behind Sprocket's ears. "But I would have gotten here no matter what. We've never missed a Christmas together, you and I, and I'm not about to start now. After all, you're my very best friend. And that's what Christmas is about—being with the ones you love the most!

"But, Sprocky," Doc added with a twinkle in his eye, "don't think I forgot to get you something! It's after midnight, so it's officially Christmas morning. And you can have your present!" He clapped his hands and went to the tree. Then he bent down, picked up Sprocket's package, and handed it to the dog. "Merry Christmas, Sprocky," Doc said. "You're the best friend a man ever had!"

Some best friend, Sprocket thought gloomily. *I don't even have a present for you.* He slowly tore apart the wrapping. Inside was a beautiful big blue bowl with Sprocket's name on it in big gold letters.

"Do you like it, Sprocky?" Doc asked. "You know, it holds almost three full cans of dog food!" Sprocket wagged his tail, but his heart wasn't in it.

Suddenly Doc squinted and walked toward the hole in the wall. He bent down and looked at something on the ground. Then he picked it up.

"Candy canes, Sprocky? Are these for me?" Doc looked a little puzzled. "Thank you, boy! What a great Christmas present! But where did you get them? We don't have any candy canes around here, do we?"

Sprocket's mouth dropped open. *Candy canes? For Doc? Where had they come from? It was a Christmas miracle!*

Sprocket never did figure it out. But he thanked his lucky bones for Doc's Christmas present. And he always remembered, too, what Doc had said. Presents were nice, but the real gift of Christmas is being with the people and dogs you love.

"Sprocket," Doc said solemnly, "I'm truly moved to be here with you on this day. Here are two dog yummies!" Doc pulled them off the tree. "Now, let me give you some dog food in your new bowl. You must be starving!"

And what had started out to be a very unmerry Christmas ended up being a wonderful Christmas after all!